Why Epossumondas Has No Hair on His Tail

WRITTEN BY

Coleen Salley

ILLUSTRATED BY

Janet Stevens

Harcourt, Inc.

Orlando   Austin   New York
San Diego   Toronto   London

Epossumondas was swinging on the porch swing one day when Skunk came pussyfooting by.

"Hi, Epossumondas," said Skunk.

"Hi, Skunk," said Epossumondas.

Skunk and Epossumondas were waving friends, not play-together friends. So they waved, and Skunk pranced on by, swishing her thick black-and-white tail.

Epossumondas kept lollygagging there on the porch, thinking and swinging, swinging and thinking. He was thinking about tails.

Skunks have thick
black-and-white tails,
he thought,

and foxes have
bushy red tails,

and even hares have fluffy
white powder-puff tails.

But my tail is just pink
and naked and funny looking.

After a while Epossumondas went inside to find his mama.

"Mama, why don't I have hair on my tail?" he asked, climbing onto her lap.

"Well, honey," Mama said, "possums haven't always had naked tails. There's an old story. A long time ago, Papapossum, your great-great-grandpa, had a fluffy little powder-puff tail just like Hare. All possums did in those days.

"Now Papapossum was a mighty smart fellow. He could fool animals much bigger than he was just by playing dead. And, oh, what a storyteller he was. But in spite of his smarts, sometimes he got himself in trouble. And this was one of those times..."

Papapossum was sleeping peacefully in his cozy bed one morning when . . .

RRRRRRR!

RRRRRRRR!

Papapossum got up. "Who's that? Is that you, Stomach, growling and groaning and kicking up a ruckus?"

RRRRR!

"You are one hungry Stomach. What's that you want? Persimmons, you say? Well, persimmons you'll get."

So Papapossum headed down the road, looking for persimmons. By and by he ran across his friend Hare, and they started jabbering and confabbing.

"What're you up to, Hare?" asked Papapossum.

"Nothin' now," said Hare. He looked tired. "I've been working hard—planting, watering, harvesting."

"Wish I had planted something," moaned Papapossum. "Stomach wishes it, too. Hear that rumbling? He's craving persimmons."

"Persimmons!" Hare said. "Mmm—sounds good to me, too. You know, Bear likes persimmons because they're sweet as honey. So he planted a whole mess of persimmon trees."

Now Hare wasn't so good at climbing trees, but he sure was good at cooking up plans. He figured he could get himself some persimmons and get Papapossum to do all the work. "I'm sure Bear would want you to have some, Papapossum," Hare said. "You can just climb up in the tallest tree and throw those persimmons right down to me. Then you take half and I'll take half. Deal?"

Before Hare finished speaking, Papapossum lit out. Hare followed close behind.

Soon Papapossum was perched on the highest branch in the highest tree, gobbling persimmon after persimmon.

"What do you say now, Stomach?" Papapossum cried. Stomach was happy, and Papapossum was happy, too. Between bites, he sang at the top of his voice. "Persimmons, 'simmons, high up in the tree. Plenty enough for Stomach and plenty enough for me!"

But Hare wasn't happy. "Hey, Papapossum, throw those persimmons down to me!"

Papapossum threw one and gobbled three. And in between gobbling, he kept right on singing "Persimmons, 'simmons, high up in the tree. Plenty enough for Stomach and plenty enough for me!"

Hare yelled louder. "C'mon, Papapossum! We made a deal!"

Papapossum threw one and gobbled five, then sang a little louder. "Persimmons, 'simmons, high up in the tree. Plenty enough for Stomach and plenty enough for me!"

Now Hare was mad. "All those persimmons for Papapossum and hardly any for me. He'll be sorry!" And Hare hightailed it down the road.

Who do you think he met on that road? That's right—Bear, coming on home.

"Hey, Bear," Hare called. "You hear that singing? I think maybe there's someone in your persimmon patch!" Then he skedaddled away.

Bear stopped . . . listened . . . and then took off, growling and snarling.

Papapossum was singing so loudly
he didn't even hear Bear coming Bear
shook the tallest tree, but Papapossum
just hung on tight and sang out,
"Three 'simmons more and then I'll go!"

Bear shook harder, but Papapossum
hung on tighter and sang out, "Two
'simmons more and then I'll go!"

Then Bear gave that tree a ferocious shake, and Papapossum hung on for dear life. Even then he sang, "Just one 'simmon more and then I'll go!"

Bear shook that tree so hard you would've thought the earth was gonna fall apart. And finally, down Papapossum dropped—down, down, down, in a shower of ripe persimmons.

The instant Papapossum touched the ground, he got his feet going and bolted for the fence as fast as a racehorse. But Bear was fast, too, and he got closer and closer.

"Stop, you persimmon-pickin' possum! I'm gonna teach you a thing or two!" snarled Bear.

Just as Papapossum slipped through the rails of the fence, Bear chomped his teeth around that little powder-puff tail. And he wasn't gonna let go—no sirree.

Bear pulled one way, Papapossum pulled the other, and that fluffy little powder-puff tail stretched. They pulled more, and it stretched more. Why, it was a tail tug-o'-war.

At last—POP! Papapossum was free, so he kept right on going and going all the way home. And Bear? He was back there at the fence with a whole mouthful of hair. Believe it or not, his teeth had stripped that powder-puff tail clean and stretched it into the longest and skinniest tail you ever did see.

Stomach wasn't quite so fond of persimmons after that. And Papapossum—he had lost that fluffy little powder-puff tail.

Now you might think that Papapossum was kind of embarrassed about his tail— it was so pink and naked and funny looking.

But he always could make something good out of something bad. It turned out that tail came in pretty handy. Papapossum found a million different ways to use it.

"And ever since then," Mama said, hugging her baby close, "no possum has ever had hair on his tail. Including you, my sweet little patootie."

RRRRRRR!

For my girlfriends, older and younger, who have been steadfast forever. Older: Sue Turner, Mary Jane Howell, Jean Nebel, and Joy Lowe. Younger: Suzanne Turner Purdin, Jean Howell Button, Lori Benton, and Jahn Lee Colling
—C. S.

For Jeannette.
We couldn't do it without you.
—J. S.

www.HarcourtBooks.com

Library of Congress Cataloging-in-Publication Data
Salley, Coleen.
Why Epossumondas has no hair on his tail/written by Coleen Salley;
illustrated by Janet Stevens.
p. cm.
Summary: Epossumondas's mother tells him a story about how his
great-great-grandfather became the first possum to have a hairless tail.
[1. Possums—Folklore. 2. Folklore.] I. Stevens, Janet, ill. II. Title.
PZ8.1.S2168Wh 2004
[E]—dc22   2003018581
ISBN 0-15-204935-5

First edition
A C E G H F D B

Manufactured in China

The illustrations in this book were done in mixed media on watercolor paper.
The display type was set in Spumoni.
The text type was set in Big Dog
Color separations by Colourscan Co. Pte. Ltd., Singapore
Manufactured by South China Printing Company, Ltd., China
This book was printed on totally chlorine-free Stora Enso Matte paper.
Production supervision by Sandra Grebenar and Ginger Boyer
Designed by Lydia D'moch